HOW TO BE A
Good Dog

dedicated to my mother, Jessie Page

HOW TO BE A
Good Dog

by Gail Page

BLOOMSBURY

NEW YORK LONDON NEW DELHI SYDNEY

Bobo tried hard to be a good dog.

He loved to hear Mrs. Birdhead say,

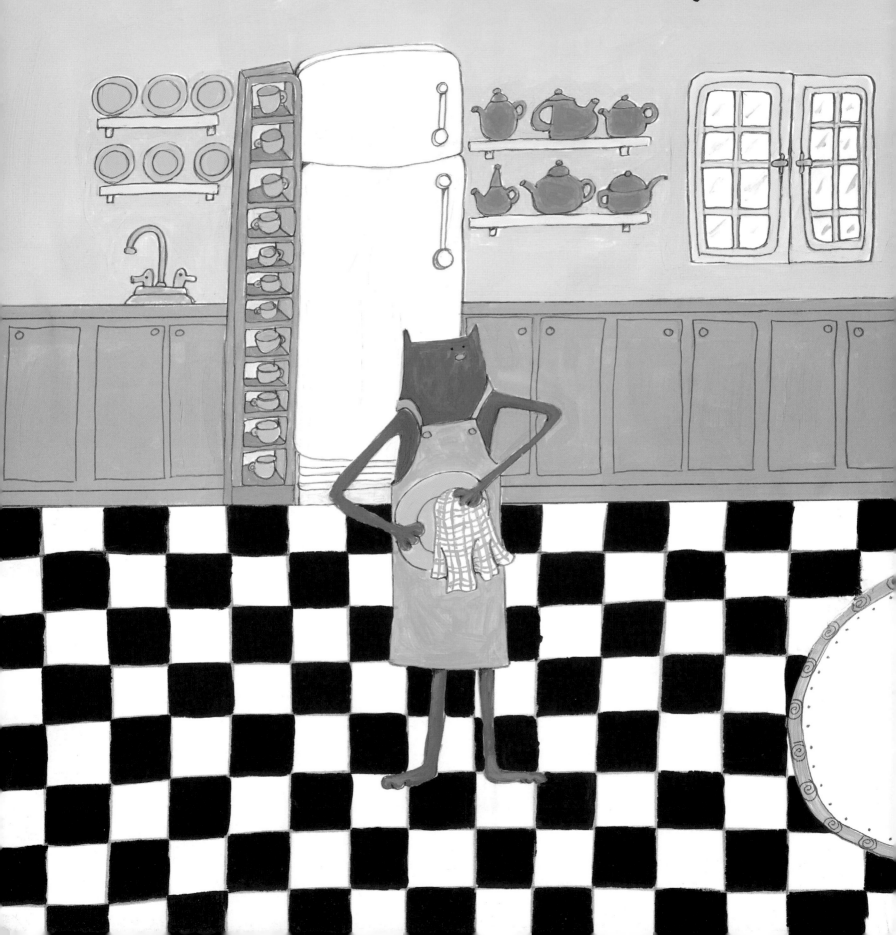

But being good was sometimes
very difficult.

bark
bark bark
bark

And when Bobo was a bad dog,
Mrs. Birdhead got strict!

Bobo missed Mrs. Birdhead.
He even missed Cat.

And much to Cat's surprise,

she missed Bobo.

How could she get him back into the house?

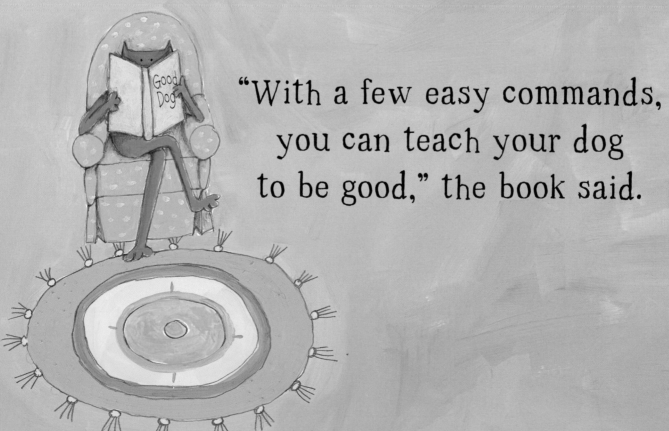

"With a few easy commands, you can teach your dog to be good," the book said.

When Mrs. Birdhead went out to run errands, Cat gave Bobo his first lesson.

They began with SHAKE.

It went very well.

Next was **FETCH.**

Then it was time to practice SIT.

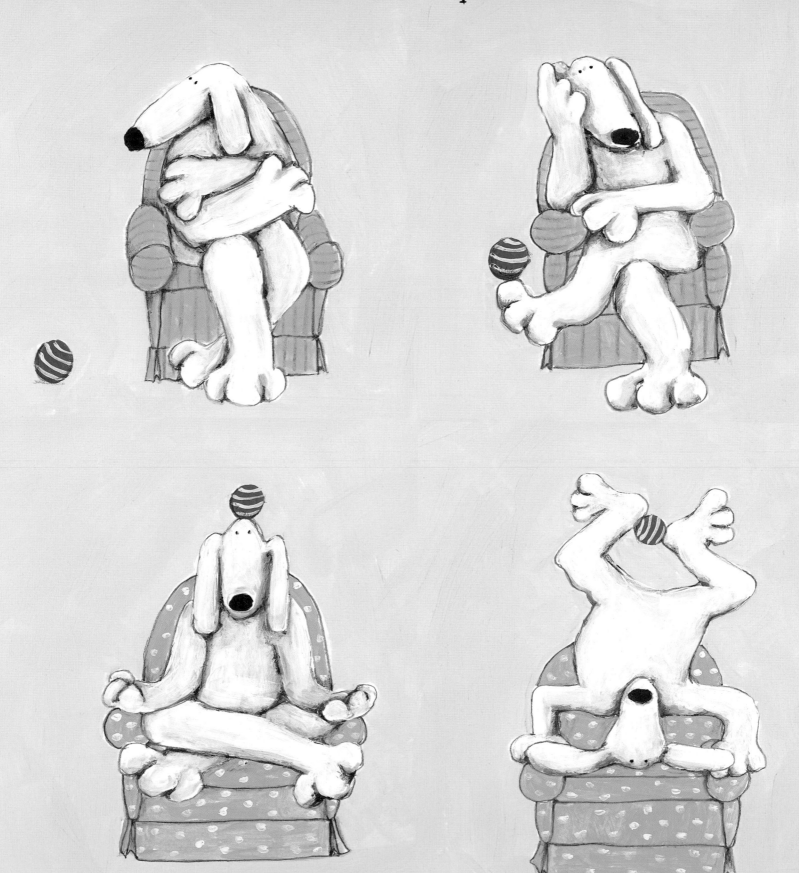

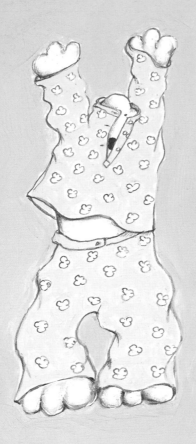

LIE DOWN was next.
It came naturally to Bobo.

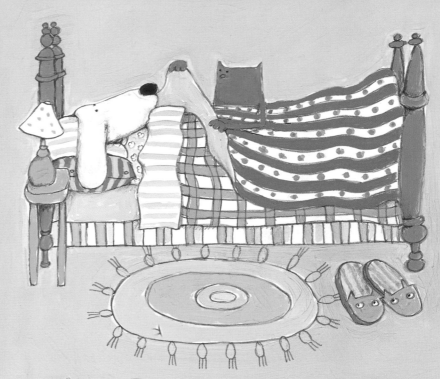

ROLL OVER
was a bit harder.

But STAY was the easiest command of all.

Well, it was easy until...

...Mrs. Birdhead came home with **the groceries!**

Cat tried to control Bobo.

But nothing worked.
Bobo couldn't wait to show
Mrs. Birdhead everything he had learned.

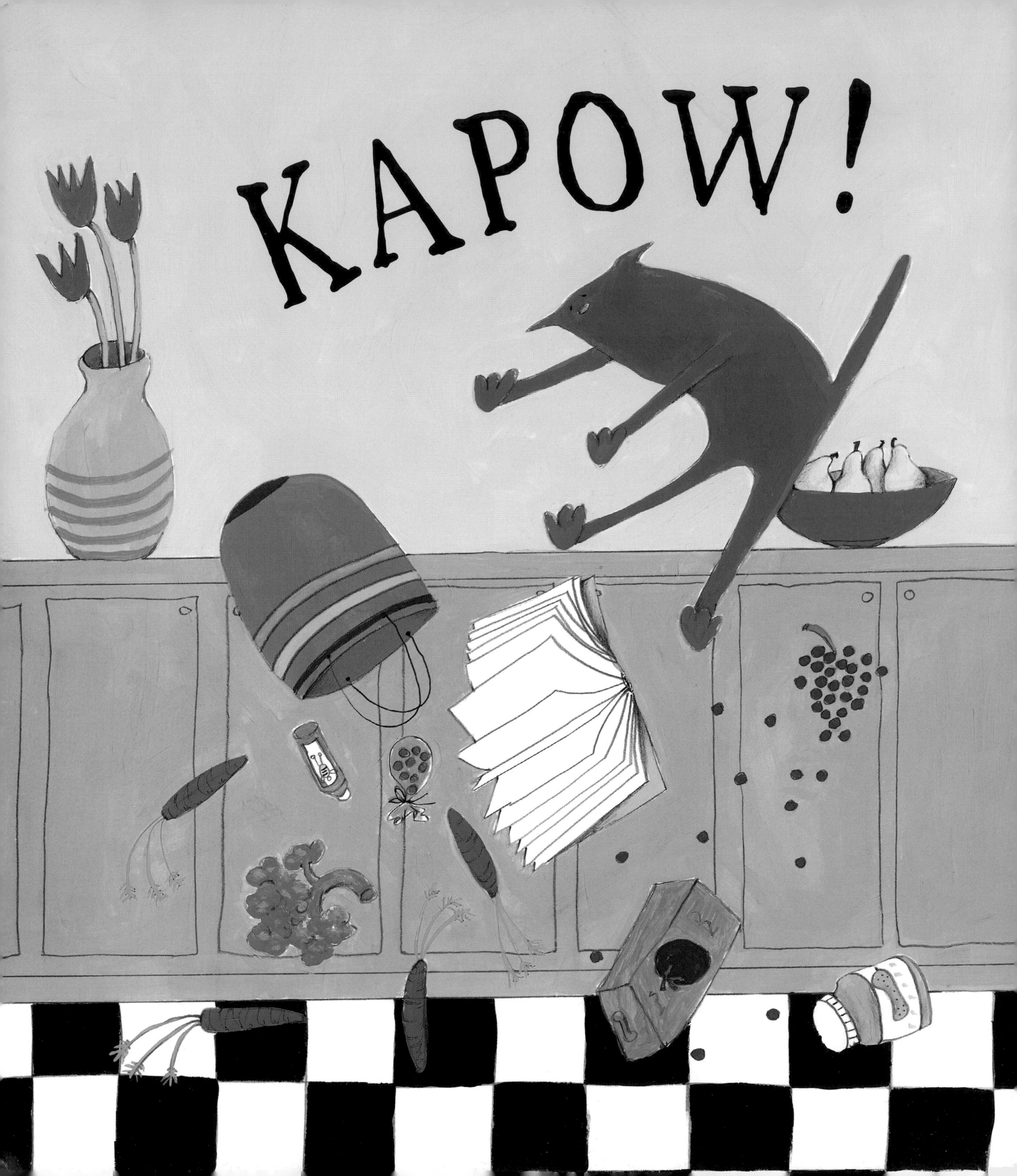
KAPOW!

But before Mrs. Birdhead could get mad, Bobo showed her how he could:

SHAKE!

SIT!

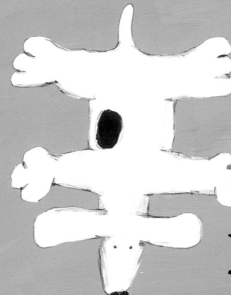

LIE DOWN!

ROLL OVER!

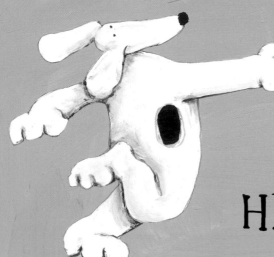

HEEL!

FETCH!

"You **ARE** a good dog, Bobo!"

And when Mrs. Birdhead
told him he was a good dog,

Bobo STAYED, and STAYED,
and STAYED.

the end

Art created with acrylics
Typeset in McKracken
Book design by Lizzy Bromley

Published by Bloomsbury U.S.A. Children's Books
175 Fifth Avenue, New York, NY 10010

The Library of Congress has cataloged the hardcover edition as follows:
Page, Gail.
How to be a good dog / by Gail Page.
p.   cm.
Summary: Cat helps Bobo the dog show Mrs. Birdhead how good he is.
ISBN-13: 978-1-58234-683-0 · ISBN-10: 1-58234-683-6 (hardcover)
[1. Dogs—Fiction. 2. Cats—Fiction.] I. Title.
PZ7.P1377 How 2006   [E]—dc22   2005057012
_____

ISBN-13: 978-1-59990-151-0 · ISBN-10: 1-59990-151-X (paperback)

Printed in China by South China Printing Company, Dongguan City, Guangdong
6 8 10 9 7 5

MIX
Paper from
responsible sources
FSC® C101537